Reptile World

Boa Constrictors

by Imogen Kingsley

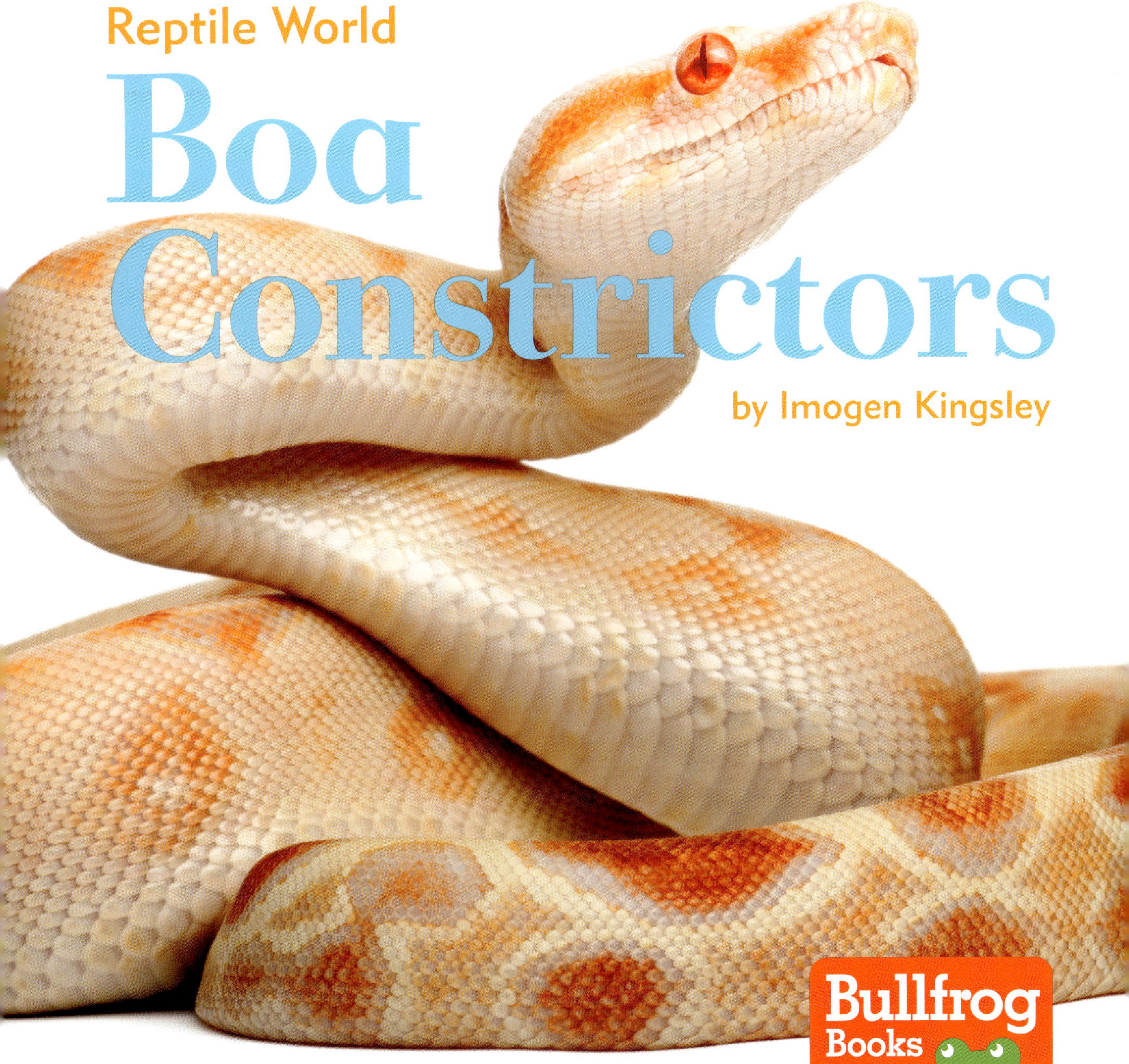

Bullfrog Books

Ideas for Parents and Teachers

Bullfrog Books let children practice reading informational text at the earliest reading levels. Repetition, familiar words, and photo labels support early readers.

Before Reading

- Discuss the cover photo. What does it tell them?
- Look at the picture glossary together. Read and discuss the words.

Read the Book

- "Walk" through the book and look at the photos. Let the child ask questions. Point out the photo labels.
- Read the book to the child, or have him or her read independently.

After Reading

- Prompt the child to think more. Ask: Have you ever seen a boa constrictor? Was it wild or in a zoo?

Bullfrog Books are published by Jump!
5357 Penn Avenue South
Minneapolis, MN 55419
www.jumplibrary.com

Library of Congress Cataloging-in-Publication Data

Names: Kingsley, Imogen, author.
Title: Boa constrictors / by Imogen Kingsley.
Other titles: Bullfrog books. Reptile world.
Description: Minneapolis, MN: Jump!, Inc., [2017]
Series: Reptile world
Audience: Ages 5-8. Audience: K to grade 3.
Identifiers: LCCN 2016048169 (print)
LCCN 2016048577 (ebook)
ISBN 9781620316641 (hard cover: alk. paper)
ISBN 9781624965418 (e-book)
Subjects: LCSH: Boa constrictor
Juvenile literature. | CYAC: Snakes.
Classification: LCC QL666.O63 K5625 2017 (print)
LCC QL666.O63 (ebook) | DDC 597.96/7—dc23
LC record available at https://lccn.loc.gov/2016048169

Editor: Kirsten Chang
Book Designer: Molly Ballanger
Photo Researcher: Molly Ballanger

Photo Credits: jbmake/Shutterstock, cover; Life On White/SuperStock, 1; Eric Isselee/Shutterstock, 3; Daniel Heuclin/Biosphoto, 4; Pete Oxford/SuperStock, 5, 6–7; Ramona Heim/Shutterstock, 5; rujithai/Shutterstock, 8–9; Patrick K. Campbell/Shutterstock, 10–11; Rosa Jay/Shutterstock, 12; Mc Donald Wildlife Photog/Animals Animals, 13, 14–15; John Daniels/SuperStock, 16; Pete Oxford/Getty, 17; Dr Morley Read/Shutterstock, 17, 18–19; Rgbe/Dreamstime, 18–19; Piotr Naskrecki/SuperStock, 20–21; fivespots/Shutterstock, 22; BlueRingMedia/Shutterstock, 23tl; amattel/Shutterstock, 24.

Printed in the United States of America at Corporate Graphics in North Mankato, Minnesota.

Table of Contents

Hide and Seek

Can you find the boa?

He is big.

He is six feet (1.8 meters) long.

Boas can be hard to see.

Their colors can match the trees.

scales

Their scale patterns help them hide.

Why do they hide?

Boas are slow.

They hide to get prey.

Here comes a bat.

A boa grabs it.
He wraps.

He squeezes.

The bat's heart stops.

The boa swallows
it whole.

Gulp!

Here comes a rat.

A boa opens its mouth.
Its jaws open wide.
It has sharp teeth.

It bites.

The rat cannot get away.

The boa squeezes.

The rat dies.

Time to eat!

Now it rests in the sun.

Parts of a Boa Constrictor

Picture Glossary

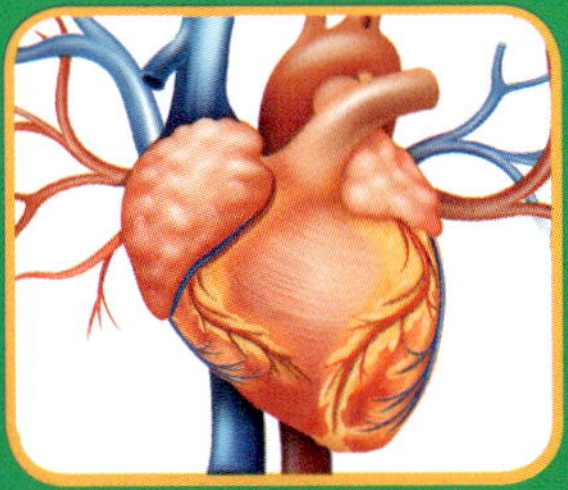

heart
The organ in the body that pumps blood.

prey
Animals that another animal hunts and eats.

pattern
Marks and designs on a snake.

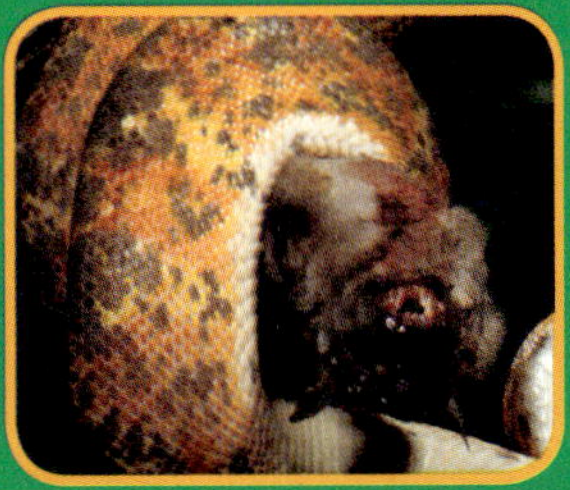

wraps
Coils around something.

Index

To Learn More

Learning more is as easy as 1, 2, 3.

1) Go to www.factsurfer.com

2) Enter "boaconstrictors" into the search box.

3) Click the "Surf" button to see a list of websites.

With factsurfer.com, finding more information is just a click away.